MATH Mini MYSTERIES

SANDRA MARKLE

ATHENEUM 1993 NEW YORK

MAXWELL MACMILLAN CANADA
TORONTO
MAXWELL MACMILLAN INTERNATIONAL
NEW YORK OXFORD SINGAPORE SYDNEY

Books by Sandra Markle

Exploring Winter
Exploring Spring
Exploring Summer
Exploring Autumn
Power Up
The Kids' Earth Handbook
Pioneering Space
Science Mini-Mysteries
Math Mini-Mysteries

Atheneum
Macmillan Publishing Company
866 Third Avenue
New York, NY 10022

Maxwell Macmillan Canada, Inc.
1200 Eglinton Avenue East
Suite 200
Don Mills, Ontario M3C 3N1

Macmillan Publishing Company is part of the Maxwell Communication Group of Companies.

First edition
Printed in the United States of America
10 9 8 7 6 5 4 3 2 1
The text of this book is set in 11 point Caledonia.
Designed by Kimberly M. Adlerman

Library of Congress Cataloging-in-Publication Data
Markle, Sandra.
    Math mini-mysteries / by Sandra Markle. —1st ed.
        p.   cm.
    Summary: Presents challenging problems that can be solved by using suggested problem-solving techniques and basic math.
    ISBN 0–689–31700–X
    1. Mathematics—Juvenile literature. [1. Mathematics.
2. Mathematical recreations. 3. Problem solving.] I. Title.
    QA40.5.M37   1993
510—dc20   92–11217

For Terry and Carol Baughn:
The value of such good friends is beyond computation

With special thanks to Shirley M. Frye, past president of the National Council of Teachers of Mathematics; Dr. Theresa I. Denman, former mathematics supervisor for Detroit City Schools and reviewer for *Instructor* magazine; Dr. Mario Salvadori, engineer and physicist, Columbia University.

On the recommendation of the expert consultants, some of the measuring activities in this book use the English scale, while others use the metric scale. Readers are encouraged to think in one scale or the other rather than to make conversions, which could be confusing. The activities have been devised under the curriculum standards developed by the National Council of Teachers of Mathematics.

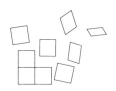

Contents

Mathematics is a tool used to tackle problem-solving situations of all kinds. For example, it can help your family figure out if your furniture will fit in a new house or apartment or it can help you decide how much food to buy for a party. Mathematics helps you define your world too, discovering and communicating the size, weight, and shape of things. With it, you can analyze information, identify patterns, and observe how things are related. Mathematics also helps you estimate or make logical guesses.

In this book, you'll discover that mathematics is a powerful tool that makes problem solving fun! You'll learn how to find out if the wind speed is just right for kite flying, search for a champion tree, enlarge a picture easily, use a map scale to find out actual travel distances, create your own "magic square" number puzzles, and lots more. You'll also discover how Mount Rushmore was carved and how cracks on these famous faces are mapped and patched. You'll compare your personal measurements to those of the Statue of Liberty, and find out how to predict when Yellowstone's Old Faithful geyser will next erupt. There are recipes to whip up, experiments to investigate, opportunities to be creative, and many puzzles to keep you thinking.

Don't miss any of the action! Before you begin, though, take time to read the problem-solving strategies on the next page.

Problem-Solving Strategies

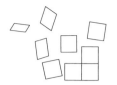

When you have a problem to solve, here are some pointers to help tackle it successfully. You may want to make a copy of this page to keep with you.

Identify the Problem

- Think about how it could be broken down into parts.

- Look for a pattern.

- Think about how you've solved similar problems.

- Collect any information that could help you solve the problem; sift out any useless information.

- State the problem in your own words so you really understand it.

- Make a chart, graph, or diagram to help you think through the problem; use objects you can manipulate to simulate the problem.

- Make an estimate of the possible solution.

Consider whether or not your solution seems reasonable.

Okay, now it's time for some action. The triangle puzzle will get you started.

How Many Triangles Can You Find?

A triangle is a closed shape that has three angles and three sides. The angles and sides may be different sizes, but a triangle always has three of each.

This design is made up of lots of triangles. Can you find them all? Start by looking for the little triangles first. Then find bigger triangles that are formed by smaller triangles. Read on for the total number of triangles in this design.

Did you find all 10 triangles? If not, look again.

Triangle Super Challenge

Now that you know the shape of a triangle and have spotted different-size triangles, try this. Arrange 8 identical wooden toothpicks so they form a three-dimensional shape made up of 4 equilateral triangles. An equilateral triangle is one that has 3 equal sides. You'll need a bit of white glue to help you complete this challenge. Check your results by looking at the solution on page 5.

Mini-Puzzles

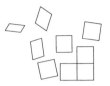

Here's a chance to use your science knowledge. You may need to search through books and encyclopedias to find clues. When you think you've discovered the solution to each of the puzzles, check yourself by reading page 7.

Puzzle #1: Multiply the number of legs an octopus has times the number of legs on a spider. Next, add the number of legs on a mosquito to the answer and subtract the number of months it usually takes for a fully developed human baby to be born. Finally, subtract the number of ears on an elephant. What's the answer?

Puzzle #2: A 2-inch-long grasshopper has been observed jumping more than a yard, or about 20 times the length of its body. What if you could jump 20 times your body length or, in other words, your height? How far would you be able to jump in one bound? Estimate the distance you could jump on a playground. Next, have a partner measure you. Then measure and mark out the starting and landing places to see how far such a jump really would take you. How close was your estimate?

Now estimate and mark how far each of these famous basketball players could leap if they could jump 20 times their height. Then measure and mark each of their starting and landing places.

Player	Height
Earvin "Magic" Johnson	81 inches
Manute Bol	91 inches
Michael Jordan	78 inches

Explain to a partner the process you used to solve this puzzle—addition, subtraction, multiplication, or division.

Puzzle #3: Bamboo, a relative of common grass, is a champion grower. It grows as much as 18 inches a day. Of course, even this speedy plant has its limits. Bamboo rarely grows to be more than 120 feet tall. At its fastest rate, how many days would it take a bamboo stalk to reach its maximum height?

Now it's your turn. Make up a puzzle to share with a friend. Be sure to solve it yourself first to see if the results are what you expected.

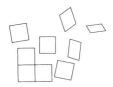

Triangle Super Challenge—Solution

When you use 8 identical toothpicks to form 4 equilateral triangles, you produce a pyramid.

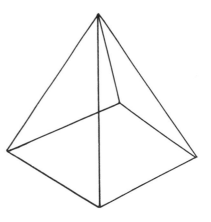

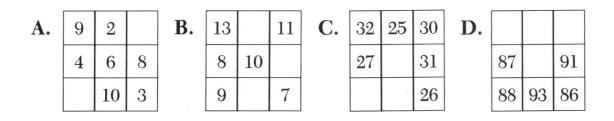

Can You Find the Magic Numbers?

These squares almost seem magical. No matter in which direction you add the numbers—vertically, horizontally, or diagonally—the sum is the same, if you add correctly. Try it for yourself. Find 33, the "magic" number sum for this square.

14	7	12
9	11	13
10	15	8

Next, find the missing numbers to complete these magic squares. Check your results on page 6.

A.

9	2	
4	6	8
	10	3

B.

13		11
8	10	
9		7

C.

32	25	30
27		31
		26

D.

87		91
88	93	86

5

Can You Find the Magic Numbers?—Solution

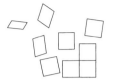

Did you discover that the strategy for solving these problems was to first determine the magic number sum for each puzzle? Then you could add together the known numbers in a row or column and subtract that sum from the magic number to find the missing number. The missing numbers for the puzzles are: A. Row 1-7, Row 3-5; B. Row 1-6, Row 2-12, Row 3-14; C. Row 2-29, Row 3-28, 33; D. Row 1-92, 85, 90, Row 2-89.

People once believed that magic number squares had religious or mystical properties because they were so mysterious. It seemed amazing that each column, every row, and even the diagonals produced the same sum. The ancient Chinese and later the Arabs, Persians, and Hindus worked to discover the secret of these magic squares. They produced even more complex ones with 5 and 9 squares to a side. Much later, Benjamin Franklin became intrigued with these puzzles and even invented a type called Franklin squares.

No one has ever been able to establish one fast rule for producing all magic squares. By studying the samples, though, you'll discover one pattern that can be used to create magic squares that have 3 numbers to a side. Each full square is made up of whole numbers that occur in sequence. For example, the square below is made up of the numbers 1 through 9. Examine the other squares to find the numbers in sequence. Then examine the order in which these numbers appear. Where is the smallest number in the sequence? The next smallest and so forth? What pattern did you discover for the placement of the numbers?

8	1	6
3	5	7
4	9	2

There are many ways to arrange the numbers in a square with 3 numbers to a side to get the same sum for every column, row, or diagonal. For example, here's one other arrangement:

9	10	5
4	8	12
11	6	7

Now build some magic squares of your own following these 2 number patterns. Then copy these leaving some of the squares blank and share the "magic square" number puzzles you created with your friends. Challenge yourself too by trying to find yet another number arrangement that you can use to build a magic square.

Here's still more magic square fun—a number sequence pattern you can use to produce a magic square with 4 numbers to a side. Try it. Like the smaller magic squares, every row column and diagonal of this bigger square will still magically produce the same sum.

8	11	14	1
13	2	7	12
3	16	9	6
10	5	4	15

Mini-Puzzles—Solution

Puzzle #1: The answer is 59. An octopus has 8 legs and so does a spider; a mosquito, like all insects, has 6 legs; a human baby usually develops for 9 months before birth; and an elephant has 2 ears.

Puzzle #2: You'll have to multiply 20 times your height in inches to see how far you could jump. (To change feet to inches, multiply the number of feet by 12—the number of inches in 1 foot. To change inches to feet, divide by 12.) "Magic" Johnson: 1,620 inches/135 feet; Manute Bol: 1,820 inches/151.66 feet; Michael Jordan: 1,560 inches/130 feet. The puzzle was solved by multiplying.

Puzzle #3: The puzzle is solved by both multiplying and dividing. First, it's necessary to convert the plant's total height in feet to inches—120 feet × 12 inches to a foot equals 1,440 inches. Then the solution is found by dividing this by the number of inches the average plant grows per day—18 inches. The answer is that the plant generally needs 80 days to reach its full height.

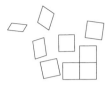

Don't Let These Snow You

When the air temperature is below freezing, water vapor forms tiny ice particles that collect around a bit of dust or a speck of sea salt. For reasons scientists don't yet fully understand, the atoms that make up the water vapor arrange themselves in orderly, 6-sided geometric shapes called *hexagons*. The more water vapor and the quicker it freezes, the more fanciful the snowflake crystal. Although the number of sides is always the same, the pattern within the ice crystal seems to be different for each one. No one knows for sure, of course, but it's often said that no two snowflakes are alike.

Like real snowflake crystals, these paper snowflakes have 6 sides and a unique form, but each has been cut in half. Can you find which halves actually belong together? Look closely for shapes and patterns of shapes that are repeated on the separated halves. When you have matched the pairs, check by looking on page 10.

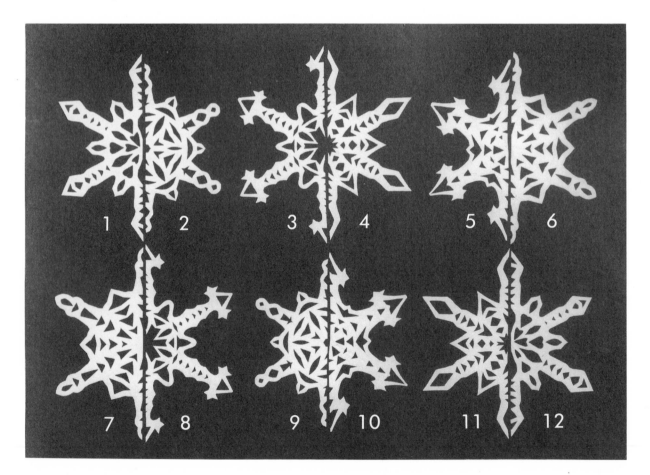

Cut Out Your Own Paper Snowflakes

Now follow the directions below to cut your own fanciful 6-sided flakes. Cut some in a variety of sizes to decorate your windows, or tie on string and hang them from the ceiling. You don't have to wait for winter or live where it gets cold to enjoy these paper snowflakes.

You'll need scissors and a sheet of 8″ × 11″ white typing paper.

1. First, fold the paper in half. Then fold it in half again so it looks like a book.
2. Notice where all the folds come together at A. Fold B over so it touches C.

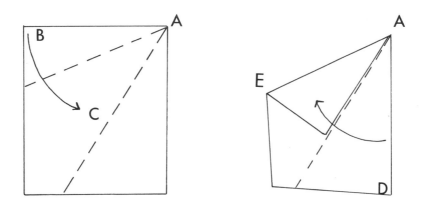

3. Fold D over to E and crease.
4. Cut the top off the folded paper at an angle.

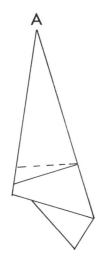

5. Cut notches along both folded edges. When you unfold the paper, you'll have a snowflake.

Just for fun, cut out seven different snowflakes and then look for special features. See if you can find at least six different special features, such as rays with round tips or a hole in the flake's center, that could be used to sort the flakes into two groups—those that have the feature and those that don't. Scientists call features that can be used to group things *attributes*.

9

Once you become skilled at observing attributes, play a mystery match game with your friends. Have each player cut out flakes until there are at least seven in the pile. Then take turns secretly thinking of an attribute and using it to group the snowflakes into two groups—those with the attribute and those without it. The challenge is to identify the secret attribute.

Real snowflakes aren't just fanciful crystals, though. Sometimes when the water vapor freezes, icy needles, hollow ice columns, snow pellets, and flat, 6-sided plates form. A lot of what is known about snowflakes is a result of the photographs taken by Wilson A. Bentley. In 1885, he discovered that he could use a camera fitted with a microscope to photograph snow, and over the next 50 years, he took more than 6,000 photographs of snowflakes.

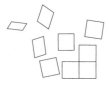

Don't Let These Snow You—Solution

The matching snowflake halves are: 1 and 12; 2 and 9; 3 and 8; 4 and 11; 5 and 10; 6 and 7.

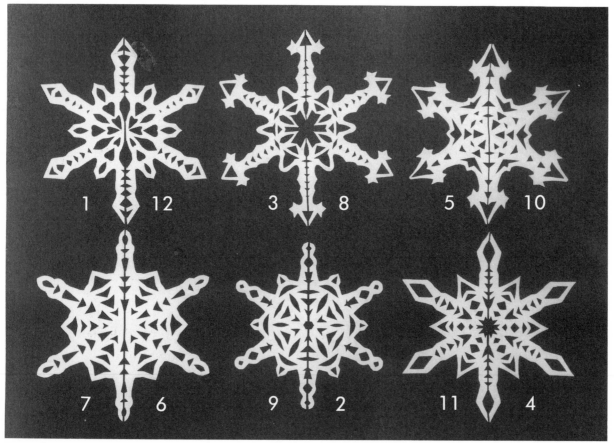

Yellowstone National Park has many geysers—about 62 percent of all the known geysers in the world. The most famous, though, is "Old Faithful," named because its eruptions can be counted on to happen with some degree of regularity. Like certain weather conditions, this geyser's eruptions can be predicted because a definite pattern has been observed and recorded. So when will Old Faithful erupt next?

Turn the page to learn how you can predict Old Faithful's eruptions.

Park rangers use a rule to predict when the next eruption is likely to begin. The rule is to time how long the geyser erupts, multiply that time by 4, and add 30 to the total. A short way to write this rule is the formula **4D + 30.**

For example, if the geyser erupted for 4 minutes, you would multiply 4 times 4 to get 16 and add that number to 30. The total in this case would be 46, meaning that the geyser could be expected to erupt again 46 minutes after it last stopped erupting. If the geyser stopped erupting at three-fifteen, the next eruption would be likely to occur at a little after four o'clock.

If the duration of the eruption was a mixed number, such as 4 minutes and 23 seconds, change the time entirely to seconds before using the formula. To do this, multiply the minutes by 60, the number of seconds in 1 minute, and add the number of seconds to this. For example, 4 minutes and 23 seconds becomes 263 seconds. After working through the formula, change the result back to minutes and seconds by dividing by 60 once again. Following our example, this would be the result: 4D + 30 (4 times 263 equals 1,052 plus 30 equals 1,082); 1,082 divided by 60 equals 18 minutes and 3 seconds.

To find the clock time that the next eruption would occur, add this time onto the time that the last eruption stopped.

Now use the formula to predict the time the next eruption of Old Faithful can be expected in each of the puzzles below. The solutions are at the bottom of the page.

Puzzle #1: It's 2:15, and Old Faithful erupted for only 6 minutes.

Puzzle #2: The geyser began erupting at 3:10 and stopped at 3:17.

Puzzle #3: After 4 minutes and 15 seconds, Old Faithful stopped erupting at 7:25.

When Will Old Faithful Erupt Next?—Solution

Puzzle #1: Old Faithful can be expected to erupt again at about 3:09.

Puzzle #2: The next eruption will begin at approximately 4:15.

Puzzle #3: Old Faithful's next eruption will start around 8:12.

Like all geysers, Old Faithful erupts because there is a heat source, a steady supply of water, and a partially watertight "plumbing system" formed by the cracks in the underground rocks in that area. Before an eruption, water seeps down into a system of interconnecting fractures, or cracks. Natural deposits of a glasslike rock material called *sinter* inside these fractures have turned them into almost watertight pipes. Water at the very bottom of the pipes is under great pressure because of the weight of the water above it. Heat from magma, or molten rock, surrounding the chamber heats the water, but because of the pressure, the deepest water must get much hotter than 212 degrees Fahrenheit, the normal boiling temperature of water, to boil. Water closest to the surface changes to steam, though, and pushes some of the water out in a small, short-lived gush. Now the pressure on the deeper water is less, and it quickly reaches the boiling point. The steam that forms gushes out, carrying with it any remaining water—often thousands of gallons. Once the system of rock pipes is nearly empty, the eruption stops, and water begins to seep back into the system to begin the cycle all over again.

Following this typical geyser pattern, an eruption of Old Faithful begins with a small gush that lasts a few minutes. Then, with a roar, steam blasts out carrying a spout of water as high as 100 to 180 feet into the air. As this water jet plays out, the eruption finishes with a few final puffs of steam.

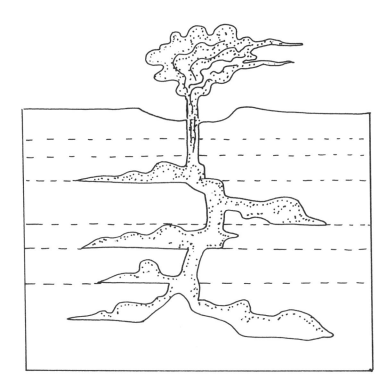

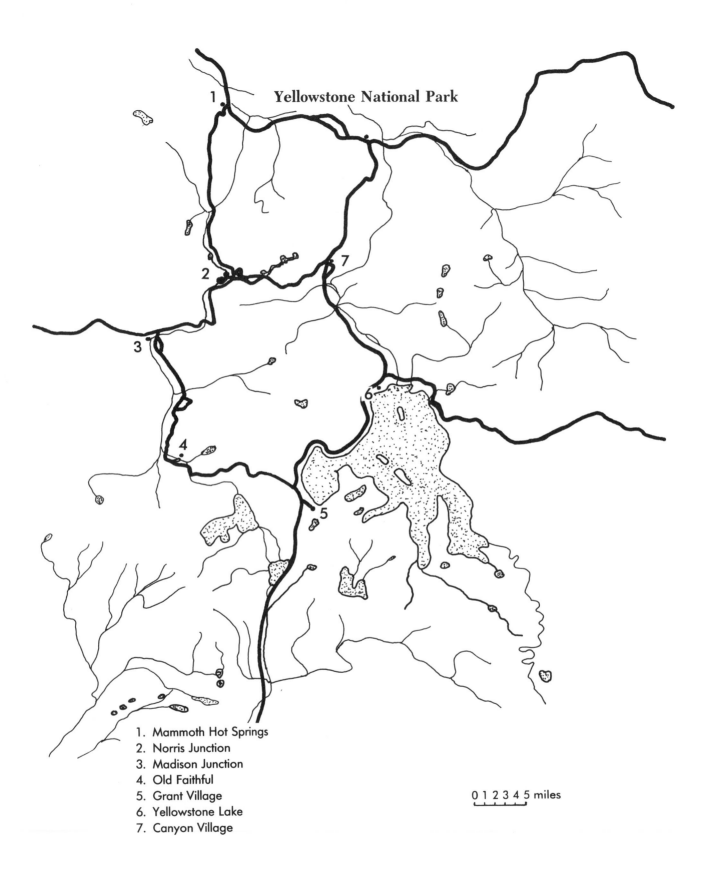

Yellowstone National Park

1. Mammoth Hot Springs
2. Norris Junction
3. Madison Junction
4. Old Faithful
5. Grant Village
6. Yellowstone Lake
7. Canyon Village

0 1 2 3 4 5 miles

Take a Grand Tour of Yellowstone

This is a scale map of Yellowstone National Park. Drawing or making something to scale means that a smaller unit of measure represents a much larger unit of measure in real life or that a bigger unit represents a smaller one. In this case, each quarter inch of line drawn on the map represents 2 miles of road.

Established in 1872, Yellowstone was the United States' first national park, but it wasn't easily accessible for visitors for many years. Then hotels and a carriage road were built. Between 1886 and 1916, most of the people who went to visit Yellowstone took what was called the Grand Tour, a special 5-day guided tour that cost $35.

As you read about the route this tour followed, use the map to find out how far the tourists traveled each day. To do this you'll need a 10-inch-long piece of light-colored string and a marking pen. First, line the string up alongside the map scale, marking each 5-mile space along its length. Then, use the string tape to measure between the points the tourists traveled each day.

The Grand Tour of Yellowstone National Park

Day	Starting and Stopping Points
1	Mammoth Hot Springs to Old Faithful
2	At Old Faithful
3	Old Faithful to Yellowstone Lake
4	Lake to Grand Canyon of Yellowstone
5	Canyon to Mammoth and take train from Livingston, Montana

Throughout the trip, the tourists traveled in 15-passenger carriages drawn by 4-horse teams. Mammoth Hot Springs, where the tour began, provided an unusual sight: Terrace Mountain. This colorful rock formation is formed by the warm water flowing over it and depositing minerals. Because this is an ongoing process, the shape and size of Terrace Mountain continue to change.

After enjoying this spectacular sight, the tourists traveled to Norris Junction. Along the way, they saw Obsidian Cliff. Obsidian, or natural glass, forms when lava cools and hardens so quickly that crystals don't have time to form. This dark volcanic cliff was called Glass Mountain by the famous mountain man Jim Bridger, who was one of the first to report the wonders of Yellowstone. The Indians valued the obsidian for making tools and for trading.

At Norris Junction, the carriages stopped, and everyone ate lunch outside under big tents at what was called Larry's Lunch Station. While there, they also visited the Norris geyser basin. This is the site of Steamboat geyser, the largest geyser in the world. It erupts, though, only on fairly rare occasions. Sometimes there are years between eruptions. In 1990, on the other hand, this geyser erupted three times. Here, there are also fumaroles, or steam vents, and mud pots, or hot springs that contain boiling, bubbling mud.

Then the carriages took the travelers to the Old Faithful geyser. Until 1904, the first night of the tour was spent in primitive lodges. Then the Old Faithful Inn was built. This huge hotel was constructed entirely of logs, and for many years it was the world's largest log structure.

After a day of sightseeing in the region around Old Faithful, the tourists journeyed to West Thumb on Yellowstone Lake. There they had the option of going by boat to the hotel at Lake (an additional $2.50) or continuing on in the carriage. At Lake, the stop for the day, tourists could walk out to see the Grand Canyon of Yellowstone. The yellow rocks in this canyon are what gave Yellowstone its name.

Other sights in the canyon area include spectacular waterfalls. Some of the tourists rented horses and rode along the canyon's rim.

On the last day of the Grand Tour, the visitors traveled by carriage back to Norris Junction, then on to Mammoth Hot Springs and off to the train station.

Grand Tour—Solution

Check your computations on how far the tour groups traveled each day against these actual mileages.

Mammoth to Old Faithful, 51 miles (Mammoth to Norris, 21 miles; Norris to Madison, 14 miles; Madison to Old Faithful, 16 miles)

Old Faithful to Lake, 38 miles (Old Faithful to Grant, 17 miles; Grant to Lake, 21 miles)

Lake to Grand Canyon of Yellowstone, 16 miles
Canyon to Mammoth, 37 miles (Canyon to Norris, 19 miles; Norris to Mammoth, 18 miles)

Y ou probably recognize this picture as Mount Rushmore, the famous memorial to democracy, showing, from left to right, presidents George Washington, Thomas Jefferson, Theodore Roosevelt, and Abraham Lincoln. Now use the graph that overlays the photo to discover which president's facial feature is identified by each set of coordinates listed below.

If you need help, check out **Reading Graphs** on the next page. And when you think you know the answers, look on page 19. Besides the solutions, you'll learn what's being done to keep natural weathering from breaking up this mountain monument.

A. 4, 7
B. 9, 4
C. 5, 6
D. 7, 4

Reading Graphs

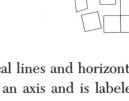

$\boxed{D}$id you notice that the graph is made up of a grid of vertical lines and horizontal lines? The starting line for all the vertical lines is called an axis and is labeled with a zero; so is the starting line for all the horizontal lines. These axes (plural of axis) may form the side and base of the graph. The numbers given for the points on a graph are called coordinates. The first number in a set of graph coordinates almost always tells the distance right or left of the starting vertical axis. The second number in a set tells the distance above or below the starting horizontal axis.

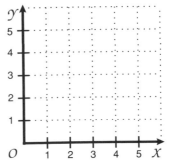

Graph coordinates are like clues to help you locate a hidden treasure. To find a mystery point on the graph, first find the vertical line indicated by the first number coordinate. Put your right index finger on the axis where this line originates. Next, find the horizontal line identified by the second coordinate and place your left index finger on the axis where this line originates. Slide your right hand up or down the vertical line and your left hand toward your right along the horizontal line. Keep moving until your two index fingers meet. The point at which your fingers meet is the exact location identified by the pair of coordinates.

You can use this locating method in reverse to "name" specific locations on a graph. To see how to do this, first find a spot on the photo of the Mount Rushmore National Memorial that you want to identify, such as Washington's chin. Put your right index finger on this spot and trace down the vertical line to where the line crosses the horizontal axis. Read the number on the horizontal axis. This is the first number of the coordinate pair, which names the point on Washington's chin. Write down this number. Next, place your finger on the point on the chin again and trace along the horizontal line to where this line crosses the vertical axis. Read the number on the vertical axis. This is the second number of the coordinate pair to identify that spot on Washington's chin on the graph.

If either finger lands between two vertical or horizontal lines, think of an invisible line running to this point. Figure out what intermediate number would correspond to this point where the line you imagined crosses the axis.

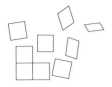

Did you correctly locate each of these presidential features: **A.** Washington's hair, **B.** Lincoln's mouth, **C.** Jefferson's eye, and **D.** Roosevelt's mustache?

Using coordinates to pinpoint specific spots on the mountain made it possible to carve the giant heads on Mount Rushmore. Gutzon Borglum, the artist responsible for the monument's creation, first built plaster models of each of the heads on a scale of 1 to 12. This meant that each inch on the model head represented 12 inches, or a foot, on the head being carved on the mountain. As each head was begun, a section of the mountain was roughly shaped into an oval. Next, a circular plate marked off in degrees was placed at the center top of the head. A mast, or tall pole with a movable boom or beam extending out from it, was anchored to the plate. You can see the mast on top of Washington's head in the photo showing the carving in progress. Precise horizontal and vertical measurements were made on the model and multiplied by 12. A degree reading on the top of the model head was used to position the boom with a degree reading on the plate on the mountain section. A plumb bob, or weight on a line, hanging from the boom was used to transfer the spot pinpointed on the model to the mountain.

First, large chunks of the granite mountain were blasted away with dynamite. Next, any remaining excess rock was removed with jackhammers to shape the features. Finally, when the carving was to within about 3 to 4 inches of the desired surface shape, shallow holes were made about 3 inches apart, using this same pinpointing technique. Then the last bits of granite were chipped off, and the surface was smoothed with a small air hammer.

Plotting Cracks

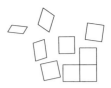

In this close-up view, you can see the cracks on the carvings. Recently, temporary spots were painted on the monument, and the location of these spots was fed into a computer. The computer then used this information to generate images scientists can use to study the cracks—how fast old ones are enlarging and where any new ones are forming.

It's natural for rock to crack in response to all sorts of stresses. Water from rain and melted snow runs into any opening; when water freezes it has more volume, or takes up more space, which enlarges the crack. Eventually this process causes chunks of rock to break away. While such weathering is normal on most mountains, it would ruin the carving on Mount Rushmore. Scientists hope that by observing cracking patterns they can discover the best way to control them there.

Cracks were always a problem on Mount Rushmore. Borglum had trouble positioning Jefferson's head because of the size and number of cracks in the granite. In fact, after he started the carving, he had Jefferson's head blasted off and began again farther to the right to avoid an especially cracked area.

To patch cracks once the carvings were complete, Borglum developed a mixture of granite dust, white lead, and linseed oil. This mixture was used to patch cracks during the annual maintenance check until 1991, when it was replaced by a new and improved silicon sealant that does a better job of keeping out water.

There is a special project under way to restore many of the facilities connected with the memorial, to build additional visitor facilities, and to fund studies to ensure the preservation of the carving itself. If you'd like more information or want to find out how you can contribute, contact the Mount Rushmore Preservation Fund, P.O. Box 1066, Rapid City, SD 57709, or call 1-800-882-0500.

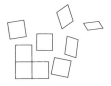

Gutzon Borglum used a grid to successfully transfer the features from the plaster model to the granite face of Mount Rushmore. Now you can use that same technique to enlarge this picture—or any picture.

First, collect four sheets of 8½″ × 11″ plain white typing paper, scissors, a ruler, and transparent tape. Measure and trim off the edges of one sheet to make an 8-inch square; use this to trim the other sheets to the same size. Fold each square in half and then in half again, being careful to keep the edges together. Unfold to reveal four 4-inch squares per sheet. Next, tape the four sheets together to form one big sheet of sixteen 4-inch squares.

Now look at just the part of the picture that appears in the upper left-hand corner box. Copy just this part in the corresponding box on your large paper sheet. Make what you draw fill up the box in exactly the same way the one in the book does. Do the same as you copy what you see in each of the other boxes.

Like Borglum, you are not only transferring the image, you're enlarging it. Notice how accurately this method of enlarging keeps all the parts of your picture in proportion. Can you figure out a way to use this method to enlarge a cartoon in the Sunday newspaper?

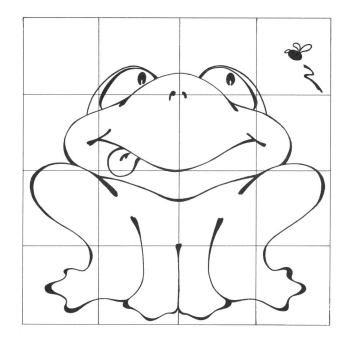

Go on a 2 Hunt

Y ou can probably easily find a 2 printed on something if you look around. How many more places can you find 2s? Carry a pencil and notepad with you for a whole day and make a note of the location every time you spot this digit. Read on for 20 sources of 2s. Next, spend a day hunting for 3s, 5s, or any other number. Which number is easiest to find? Hardest? Challenge a friend to see who can find the most of a special number in a day.

Here are some places you could look for 2s: a scoreboard, dress-size label, price list at a fast-food restaurant, calculator keypad, page number in a book, roadside mileage sign, clock face, car license plate, house address, zip code on a letter, shoe size, phone number in a phone book, sign displaying the temperature, number of gallons on the gas pump, television channel dial, telephone dial, car speedometer, elevator floor panel, team player's jersey, a recipe, grocery store receipt.

ind the pattern in this display of fruits and vegetables. What are the next 6 items that should be used to continue the pattern? Check your solution on page 25.

Here's a clue to solving this puzzle—start at the first food item on the left and work your way to the right. Look closely and count.

A sequence is a pattern in a series. Here are some more to challenge you. Look for the pattern in each of the following shape sequences and decide what the next 6 shapes should be. Draw them in order on a piece of paper. Then look on page 25 to check yourself.

1. ▲▲●■▲▲●■▲

2. ◖◗▲◖◗▲◖◗

3. ■◗◖■◗◖▲◖▲■◗◖▲■◗◖

Create Sequence Jewelry

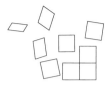

Okay, here's a chance to use your patterning skills artistically to create a necklace you can wear yourself or give as a gift. Look at the different shapes of macaroni shown below. Think about how you would use these shapes to create a pattern for a necklace. Patterns can be any length before they repeat.

Now, if possible, make the necklace you planned. You'll need:

- a piece of yarn or string about 24 inches long
- macaroni pieces like those shown in the picture (available at grocery store)

First, follow your plan to prepare one sample pattern for your necklace. Next, stretch out the string and lay the pattern you prepared beside the string. How many complete sets of your pattern will you need to complete the necklace? How many of each piece will you need? Remember you'll be leaving about 2 inches of string exposed at either end in order to tie the ends together.

To begin, tie one end of the string to the middle of a pencil. This will keep the pieces from slipping off while you work. Then thread the macaroni pieces onto the string one part of the pattern at a time. You can tie on pieces that don't have holes through them. When one entire pattern has been completed, repeat it, starting with the very first part of the pattern once again. Keep on until only about 2 inches of the string remain and remove the string from the pencil. Tie the 2 ends of the necklace together.

You could also make sequence bracelets. Use a piece of quarter-inch elastic that's as long as the circumference, or distance around your wrist, plus 4 inches. That extra length will let you tie the ends together and still slip the finished bracelet easily over your hand.

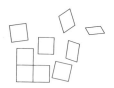

The next 6 items are: 3 strawberries, 1 apple, 3 strawberries, a bunch of grapes, 2 carrots, and 3 strawberries.

1. △ ● ■ ▣ △ △ ●

2. D ◀ ◖ D ◖ △ ◖

3. ■ ◖ ◀ △ ◖ ■ ◖ ◖

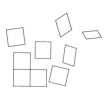

Is the Wind Right for Kite Flying?

It's fun to fly a kite, particularly one as beautiful as this faceted box kite. According to kite designer Debra Lumpkin, it's ideal kite-flying weather when the winds are blowing between 5 and 15 miles per hour. So is today a good day to fly a kite where you live? You can check by making a special instrument called an anemometer, which measures wind speed. While there are a number of different types of anemometers, the directions that follow are for one that you can easily make and use.

You'll need:

- plastic protractor (available at stores that sell school supplies)
- 12 inches of string
- Ping-Pong ball
- pushpin
- screw eye
- 12-inch ruler
- clear packaging tape

- Use the pushpin to poke a hole in the Ping-Pong ball. Turn the screw eye into this hole until it's securely anchored. Thread one end of the string through the loop in the screw eye and tie a knot.
- Place the free end of the line straight across the middle of the flat edge of the protractor and tape in place.
- Lay the protractor on the ruler so the flat edge matches the ruler's edge. Tape the protractor to the ruler.

To check the wind speed, take the anemometer outdoors, hold it by the end of the ruler opposite the protractor, and face into the wind. Sight along the upper straight edge of the ruler and protractor to be sure you're holding it straight, and check what number the string is stretched across on the curve of protractor. Find that number in the first column of the chart below and look at the wind speed in the column directly next to it. Always take at least 3 wind speed readings and figure an average. To do that, add the 3 speeds together and divide by 3. Averaging will help you be sure you weren't just reading a wind gust.

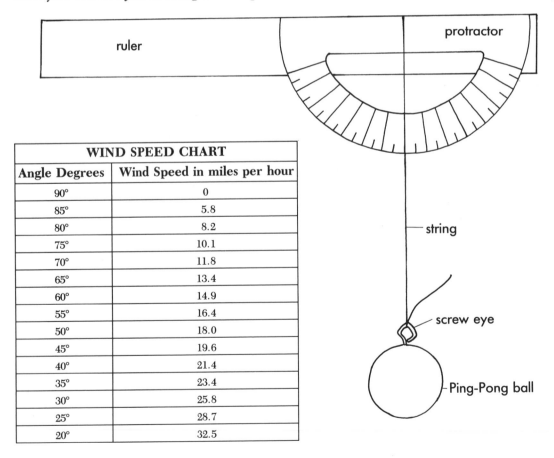

WIND SPEED CHART	
Angle Degrees	**Wind Speed in miles per hour**
90°	0
85°	5.8
80°	8.2
75°	10.1
70°	11.8
65°	13.4
60°	14.9
55°	16.4
50°	18.0
45°	19.6
40°	21.4
35°	23.4
30°	25.8
25°	28.7
20°	32.5

What time of day—morning, midday, or evening—is the wind most likely to be just right for kite flying where you live? You probably don't know for sure, but now that you have an anemometer you can find out. Be sure to check the wind speed in the morning, at midday, and in the evening on at least 3 different days for 3 weeks.

March has the reputation of being the best kite-flying month. Keep checking the wind speed all year, and you'll discover if this month really does have the best kite-flying weather where you live.

Do You Know a Champion Tree?

As of 1990, this is the biggest American beech tree in the United States. Of course, you may know of one that is even bigger that could displace this champion. Or you may know a champion of another species, or type, of tree. Turn the page to find out how you can tell.

This champion American beech is growing in Ashtabula County in Ohio. It's about 130 feet tall, and its circumference, or the distance around its trunk 4½ feet above the ground, is 222 inches.

Official Rules for Tree Contenders

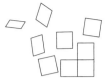

The American Forestry Association (AFA) began registering big trees in 1940 and set guidelines for determining record holders. Pick a tree you think could be a contender. Use books on tree identification to find out what kind of tree it is. A librarian can help you find these. Then follow the official guidelines below to determine if it really is a champ.

First, you'll need to check three measurements: 1) the tree trunk's circumference, or distance around; 2) the tree's vertical height; and 3) the average crown spread, meaning how far its branches extend out from the trunk in any direction. The tree's circumference needs to be measured as close as possible to 4.5 feet above the ground. If there is a branch at that height, measure the trunk just below the branch. For a really fat tree trunk, you'll need to use a string to go around the tree and then stretch this out on the ground and measure how long the string is with a yardstick.

There are special tools for measuring the height of a tree, but you can estimate the height with just a pencil and a measuring tape. First, hold a brand-new unsharpened pencil at arm's length so it's vertical. Lock your elbow to keep your arm straight and stand—facing the tree—directly in front of the trunk. Slowly back away from the tree until you can sight the tip of the treetop over the top of the pencil and the base of the tree along the opposite end of the pencil. Turn the pencil until it's horizontal, pointing at the tree, and lay it straight down on the ground at the tip of your toe. Measure from the end of the pencil pointed at the tree to the tree's trunk. That distance is approximately the height of the tree.

Finally, you'll need to measure the average crown. To do this, first walk around the tree, placing markers directly beneath the outermost tips of the branches. Pretend you can draw a line straight through the center of the trunk and decide which two markers are farthest apart on opposite sides of the tree. Next, measure the distance between the two points, including the approximate distance through the tree's trunk. Also find the two markers that are closest together on opposite sides of the tree and measure the distance between

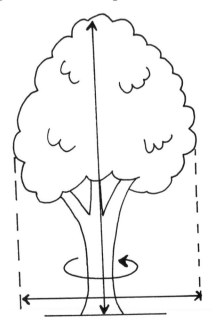

them. Add these two measurements together and divide by 2 to find the average crown spread. Then divide this average by 4 to find the number you'll need to compute the tree's total points when submitting it as a contender to the American Forestry Association's National Big Tree Registry.

The AFA computes one representative number for each tree by adding together the tree trunk's circumference in inches, its height in feet, and one-fourth of its crown spread in feet. The AFA also requires the following information about any tree being considered for its national registry of champions:

1. the correct scientific name—genus and species—of the tree; a librarian can help you find this
2. the specific location of the tree
3. the date the tree was measured and who did it
4. the name and address of the tree's owner
5. a photograph of the tree and date photographed
6. description of the tree's physical condition
7. the name and address of the person nominating the tree

If you want to submit a tree for consideration, send the information and photo to the National Big Tree Program, American Forestry Association, P.O. Box 2000, Washington, DC 20013. You can also request a copy of the *National Register of Big Trees* (available for a small fee) for a complete list of current champions. This list also includes the names of tree species for which no champion has yet been named. You could be the one to find a champ!

What Is It?

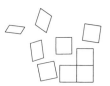

This is actually a highly magnified view of the covering of something that's very familiar. Can you guess what it is? Here are some clues to help you guess.

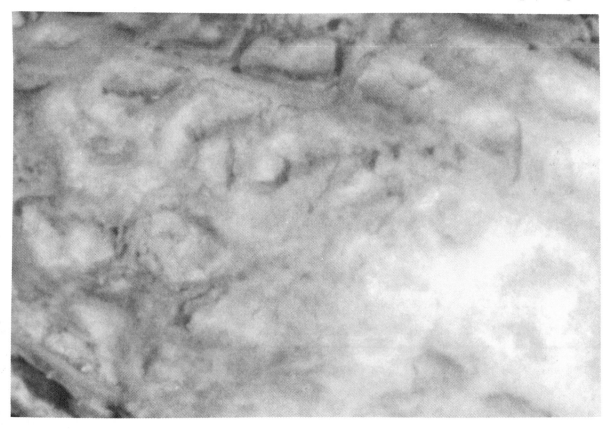

When you think you know the identity of this mystery item, check the solution on page 33. Then try the additional challenges.

- It's the seed of a plant that develops underground.
- It's nearly 50 percent oil.
- It's a popular food and very nutritious because it's high in protein.
- It's also widely used in soaps, shampoos, face powder, paint, and many other products.
- Although it originally came from South America, Georgia in the United States is now the leading grower.

$\mathbb{D}$ oes it seem hard to believe that you and this moth have something in common? Take a close look and see if you can figure out in what way the two of you are alike. When you think you know, read on.

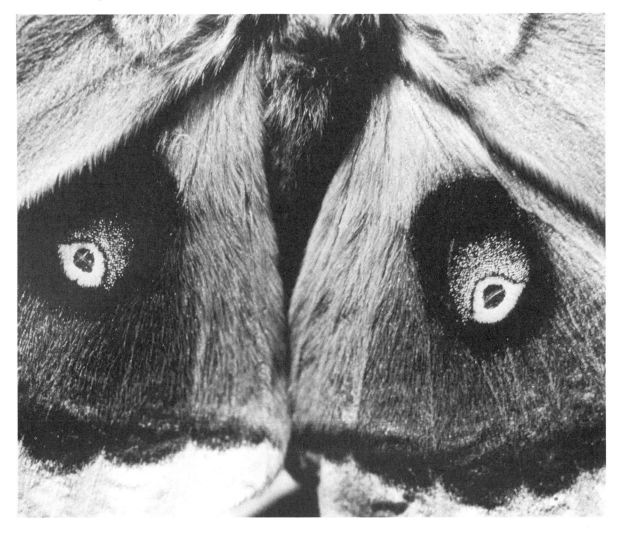

Did you notice that, like you, the moth has a right side that almost exactly matches its left side? Like you, the moth also has a definite middle line. This kind of balanced arrangement of parts on either side of a center line is called bilateral symmetry. Anything, including you and the moth, that can be separated into two equal halves by drawing a line vertically down through the middle has bilateral symmetry.

Look at yourself in the mirror. Of course, you were probably already aware of the fact that most of your body parts come in a matched set—two eyes, two ears, two shoulders, two arms, and so forth.

Some things have another kind of symmetry called radial symmetry in which there isn't a definite right or left. The parts radiate out in all directions from the center. A starfish is an example of an animal with radial symmetry.

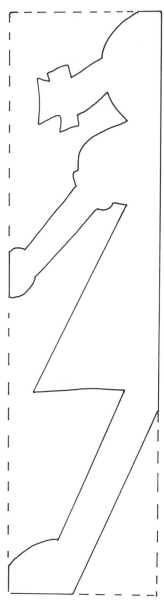

Look around you. How many things can you find that have bilateral symmetry? Radial symmetry?

Now use symmetry to create a whole chain of matched people. You'll need a plain sheet of paper— preferably 8½″ × 14″—a pencil, and scissors.

First, fold over about 2 inches on one end of the paper. Next, take this end and fold it back 2 inches from the first, creating a second 2-inch fold. Repeat this accordion folding until you reach the other end

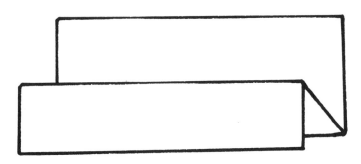

of the sheet of paper. Don't worry if the last folded section isn't 2 inches wide.

Make a freehand copy something like this simple figure of a boy or girl, making sure the hands and shoes extend out to the very edge of the folded paper.

Cut along the lines, and when you're finished, unfold the pattern. Notice the center line on each little figure and the distinct bilateral symmetry.

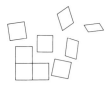

What Is It?—Solution

Did you guess that this is a peanut?

Now here's another challenge. Collect a handful of peanuts in their shells. (You can buy a bag of peanuts at a grocery store.) Pick out one. No two peanuts have shells with identical shapes and patterns. Your challenge is to get to know yours well enough to pick it out of the whole handful of peanuts.

First, you'll want to investigate your peanut's special attributes, or characteristics. Draw a picture of the peanut, showing any marks, bumps, or cracks that might help you identify it. Next, measure its length and circumference, or distance around, at its fattest and skinniest points. If you have access to a kitchen scale or postal scale, weigh the peanut too. You could even build a model out of modeling clay.

When you're ready for the test, place your peanut in a pile of other peanuts and mix them together. Then look for yours.

If you did a careful job of checking out attributes, you'll be able to find your own special peanut easily. By weighing, measuring, and looking for distinguishing features, you'll be able to make sure you really have recovered your very own peanut.

Feeding Time at the Zoo

There are more than eleven thousand animals living at the Cincinnati Zoo in Cincinnati, Ohio. Below are the costs of one day's food to feed just the tigers, walruses, and gorillas.

How much would it cost to purchase food for these three kinds of animals for a week? A month? How much just to buy vegetables for a year?

Food Costs

Meat $180
Vegetables $300
Fish $150

An adult gorilla like Mahari is a herbivore, or plant eater. She'll eat about 60 pounds of food each day. Baby Alice will continue to nurse until she's between 12 and 18 months old.

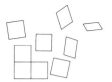

Feeding Time at the Zoo—Solution

Now you know it costs a lot to feed all the tigers, walruses, and gorillas at the Cincinnati Zoo: $4,410 per week; $17,640 per month; $109,500 just for vegetables for an entire year. So you probably won't be surprised to learn that the zoo's annual food bill for all of the animals is about $520,000.

The Cincinnati Zoo's grocery list includes huge quantities of fresh fruits and vegetables, liver, meats, and eggs. The eggs are hard-boiled and then peeled and chopped up. Only adult ostriches can eat eggs with their shells on. The ostrich keepers toss the eggs to the birds, which swallow them whole.

In addition to this more common fare, the zoo must also buy mealworms, rats, and crickets in assorted sizes. Newly hatched "pin-head" crickets are for small eaters like the poison arrow frogs. Bigger frogs get bigger crickets. Many birds need full-grown crickets. But the really big eaters are the elephants. One week's order for the elephant house includes 18 bales of timothy hay, 15 bales of alfalfa hay, and 25 50-pound bags of "exotic ruminant diet" (similar to what farmers feed their cows).

Then there are the fussy eaters that need special food. The zoo's colony of vampire bats, for example, won't drink anything but fresh blood. Luckily, that food is contributed by a local slaughterhouse.

If you'd like to get a taste of what some of the animals are eating at the zoo, try the two recipes on the next page.

Bruiser and Aituk are walruses. In the wild, walruses often eat mollusks such as clams, but at the zoo, they dine mainly on herring and squid. Their funny-looking whiskers help them "feel" out food when they brush against it underwater.

This is Tapi, one of 8 rare white tigers at the Cincinnati Zoo. There are about 160 white tigers in the whole world. White tigers are just like other tigers except a genetic variation makes their fur white and their eyes blue.

Favorite Salad

Many of the animals, such as the opossums and mice, enjoy a salad. Mix together a ¼ cup of each of the following fruits and vegetables cut into bite-size chunks: oranges, carrots, bananas, pineapple, lettuce, and apples. Toss in a small handful of seedless grapes and stir in 3 tablespoons of orange juice to keep the bananas and apples from darkening. The zoo often adds fresh green beans too.

Zoo Bread

This nutritious bread is whipped up daily for the gorillas. To cook some for yourself, you'll need 2 cups uncooked long grain rice, 1 cup raisins, and ½ cup corn syrup or honey. Mix the ingredients together in a bowl and add enough water to cover. Let the mixture sit overnight. Add the amount of water indicated on the rice package for cooking 2 cups of rice and bring the mixture to a boil. Turn down the heat and simmer until the rice has absorbed the water and is tender. Stir in 2 well-beaten eggs. Bake in a greased and floured loaf pan at 300 degrees for 2½ hours.

Many zoos have special adoption programs that let you contribute money to help feed one or more of the animals. Check with your local zoo or write to Adopt Program, Zoological Society of Cincinnati, Department 919, Cincinnati, OH 45269, to find out more about this program at the Cincinnati Zoo.

How Acid Is Your Rain?

People are concerned because acid rain is decreasing the amount of food crops yield. In streams, ponds, and lakes, it kills fish, frogs, and insects too. It also damages buildings. To find out what makes rain acid and how acid rainfall is in your area, read on.

Acids are chemicals that share the same special features when dissolved in water: a sour taste, the ability to break down proteins and metals, and the ability to conduct electricity. Of course, only very weak acids, such as the citric acid in orange juice or the tannic acid in tea, are safe to taste. Weak acids occur naturally in many of the fruits and vegetables you eat. Your body also produces a somewhat stronger acid in your stomach to help break down the protein in the foods you eat.

An acid's strength is measured by a special value called the pH scale. The scale goes from 0 to 14. The lower the number value the solution registers, the stronger the acid.

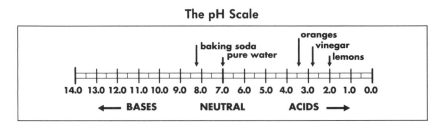

The pH Scale

baking soda
pure water
oranges
vinegar
lemons

14.0 13.0 12.0 11.0 10.0 9.0 8.0 7.0 6.0 5.0 4.0 3.0 2.0 1.0 0.0

← BASES   NEUTRAL   ACIDS →

If something registers a value higher than 7, it's considered a base, or alkaline. If the value is exactly 7 on the pH scale, the substance is said to be neutral, or neither an acid nor a base. The pH scale is a logarithmic scale, which means that every 1-unit drop on the scale represents an acidity level that is 10 times greater than the one before. For example, if the acid rain level is pH 4, it's 10 times more acidic than rain, which measures pH 5.

Rain is normally slightly acid—about pH 5.6 to 6.0—because carbon dioxide gas, which normally occurs in air, combines with rainwater to form carbonic acid. Pollutants rise into the air, especially the chemicals produced by burning coal in factories or power plants and the exhaust from cars and trucks. When these combine with the water in the air, the acid level of the precipitation—snow, sleet, and hail, as well as rain—is stronger than normal. Even fog may sometimes be acidic. According to a National Wildlife Federation's report, the most extremely acid rain recorded fell in Wheeling, West Virginia. Its pH measured only 1.5, which means that it was even more acidic than vinegar, which has a pH of 2.8. (Remember, the lower the pH value, the stronger the acid.)

From March 1988 through December 1990, individuals and groups across the United States participated in the Citizens' Acid Rain Monitoring Network. Following careful guidelines so that all the rain was collected and measured in the same way, these monitors reported the average acidity of rainfall in their community to the National Audubon Society. Then these data were compiled to produce a state average and were used to generate an acid rainfall map.

Here are the maps for August for the first and last year of the study. If data were reported for your state, when was the acid level highest? Lowest? Think back over the past three years. What conditions might have affected the level of acidity in your rainfall? Ask your parents or other adults to help you think of reasons.

Look at the whole United States. What areas consistently seem to have rainfall that is strongly acidic? Check encyclopedias to find out about these states. What factors could be causing those regions to have a bigger problem with acid rain? Look for information about the types of industries in each state. Are there big cities noted for lots of traffic problems? Auto emissions contribute to air pollution.

NATIONAL AUDUBON SOCIETY
Citizens' Acid Rain Monitoring Network

State pH Average for August 1988

State pH Averages for August 1990

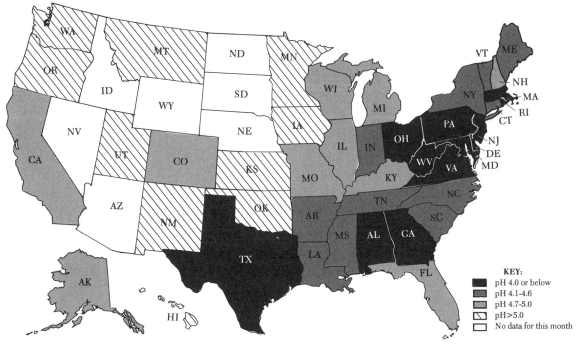

KEY:
- ■ pH 4.0 or below
- ▨ pH 4.1-4.6
- ▨ pH 4.7-5.0
- ▨ pH>5.0
- □ No data for this month

Fast Facts about Acid Rain

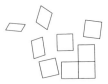

- Normal rain is slightly acidic, with a pH reading of about 5.6. That's not strong enough to hurt plants. In fact, it helps them grow. This normal acid level will cause minerals in rocks and soils to slowly dissolve in the rainwater so they can be carried down to plant roots. Plants need these dissolved minerals to grow.
- Rains that are more strongly acid have an unhealthy effect on plant and animal life in lakes and streams. According to the National Wildlife Federation, at a pH of 5.5, bottom-dwelling bacteria, which promote normal decomposition, begin to die, and leaf litter and debris build up on the bottom. If the level drops to pH 3.5, most fish, frogs, and many insects die, but the water still appears clear and blue.
- Studies show that acid rain damages bush beans, radishes, and soybeans; causes beets, carrots, and broccoli to have reduced yield; and makes the skins on apples spotted. Lettuce and spinach leaves are also damaged.
- Summer rains are usually the most acid. This is true because it generally rains less often during the summer, allowing more time for pollutants to collect in the atmosphere before rains clean the air. The increased use of cars for summer travel and of power plants to produce electricity for air-conditioning also contributes to the higher levels of pollution in the atmosphere during the summer.

Test the pH of Your Local Rain

First, you'll need a glass or plastic container with a large mouth to collect rainfall. You'll also need a pH test kit, which is inexpensive and available through stores that sell aquarium supplies. This kit will only be able to test for a limited pH range—usually pH 4.8 through pH 7. When the testing solution is added, the water will change color depending on the pH level and you'll be able to compare this color to the color on a chart that is included with the package.

After you've collected some rain, follow the package directions to test the pH level. Although you'll only be able to measure moderate levels of acidity, you'll still be able to get an idea about how acid the rain is in your community.

For information on an inexpensive acid rain testing kit capable of measuring a much broader pH range—pH 2 to pH 9—contact Hawk Creek Laboratory, Inc. R.D. 1, Box 686, Simpson Road, Glen Rock, PA 17327; 1-800-637-2436.

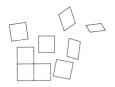

You and the Statue of Liberty

The chart below shows some of the Statue of Liberty's measurements. Copy it onto a sheet of notebook paper. Next, measure each of your features listed on the chart and record this information. Then, subtract your measurements from Miss Liberty's measurements to see how much bigger she is. Remember, your measurements and those for Miss Liberty must be in the same unit, such as centimeters, in order to be able to subtract.

Features	Statue of Liberty	You	Difference
Mouth (width)	91 centimeters		
Nose (length)	1.37 meters		
Eyes (distance across)	76 centimeters		
Index finger (length)	2.43 meters		
Height (head to toe)	33.83 meters		
Waist (side to side)	10.67 meters		
Right arm (shoulder to hand in grasping position)	12.80 meters		
Fingernail	33 centimeters by 25 centimeters		

While you're comparing, take another look at the head of George Washington on Mount Rushmore (page 19). This figure is 18 meters from chin to forehead. The president's nose is 6 meters, his eyes are 3.3 meters across, and his mouth is 5.4 meters wide. If the entire figure had been carved using this scale, President Washington would be 139.5 meters tall. How do you and Miss Liberty compare to these mountainous measurements?

Building Miss Liberty

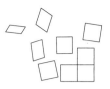

Now that you know how big the Statue of Liberty is, you probably won't be surprised to learn that constructing a framework for this giant lady was an engineering challenge. First, the basic shape of the statue was created in much the same way as the Mount Rushmore carving. Frédéric-Auguste Bartholdi, the French artist who designed the statue, began by making a plaster model one-fourth the size of the finished statue. Then, separate parts of Miss Liberty, such as the torch, toes, and head, were created out of sheets of copper one at a time. This was accomplished by measuring many points on the model and transferring these dimensions in scale to the finished form. A latticework of wooden strips supported the copper and allowed the metalworkers to shape the folds and contours.

Developing a permanent supporting framework for the completed statue was a bigger challenge. The original plan proposed by Eugène Viollet-le-Duc was to build a honeycombed framework inside the statue's hollow copper shell and fill each of the compartments this created with sand. But when Viollet-le-Duc died before being able to carry out his plans, Bartholdi turned to Alexandre-Gustave Eiffel to do the job. Eiffel was already famous for his new bridge-building ideas. He developed a system of iron columns held together by nine levels of horizontal beams and diagonal braces for Miss Liberty's skeleton. He further arranged for a secondary framework of lighter iron belts that would outline the statue's shape and be connected to the metal skin by pieces of copper. An insulating material was inserted between the iron and copper because when these two metals are in contact with each other, a chemical reaction occurs that damages the metal.

Here, you can see inside the statue. Although the Statue of Liberty held up well for her first 100 years, studies then showed some damage. A thorough renovation effort replaced the many rusted support pieces with new ones made from heavier metal. The original ironwork was left only in Miss Liberty's heel as a record for future generations.

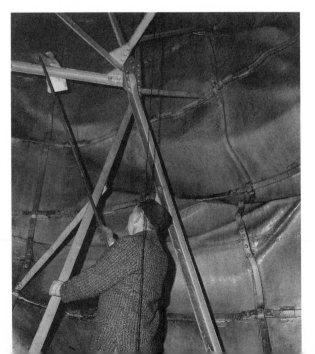

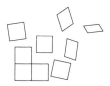

The chart below shows the 1990 American Kennel Club's top 10 dog breeds, based on the number of individual dogs of each breed that have been registered. The list is out of order, though. On a sheet of notebook paper, arrange the breeds in order from the one with the most dogs to the one with the fewest. The correct order is in the paragraph below. Then follow the directions to compile a data base about these popular breeds. You'll also discover a way to sort this information that you could use to sort any data.

Breed	Number of Dogs Registered
dachshund	44,470
poodle	71,757
beagle	42,499
rottweiler	60,471
golden retriever	64,848
cocker spaniel	105,642
German shepherd	59,556
Labrador retriever	95,768
miniature schnauzer	39,910
chow chow	45,271

The top 10 dog breeds: cocker spaniels, Labrador retrievers, poodles, golden retrievers, rottweilers, German shepherds, chow chows, dachshunds, beagles, miniature schnausers.

To prepare the data base, you'll need to find out some key facts about each of the top 10 dog breeds. Make a copy of the data sheet on the next page for each dog, and check books and encyclopedias to discover the yes or no answers to each question.

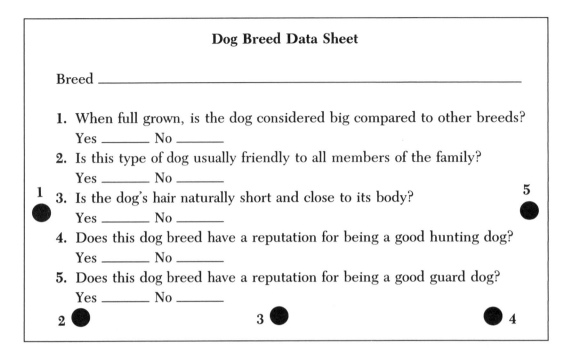

Dog Breed Data Sheet

Breed _____

1. When full grown, is the dog considered big compared to other breeds?
   Yes _____ No _____
2. Is this type of dog usually friendly to all members of the family?
   Yes _____ No _____
3. Is the dog's hair naturally short and close to its body?
   Yes _____ No _____
4. Does this dog breed have a reputation for being a good hunting dog?
   Yes _____ No _____
5. Does this dog breed have a reputation for being a good guard dog?
   Yes _____ No _____

Next, you'll need ten 3″ × 5″ index cards, a hole punch, scissors, a pen, and a pipe cleaner (available at stores selling craft supplies) or knitting needle. Write the name of each breed on the center of one of the cards. Write the numbers 1 through 5 around the edge of one card as shown in the diagram and punch a hole next to each number. Use this card as a guide to punch holes in the same spots on each of the other cards. Number the holes on each card as you did on the guide card. Check your data sheet for the answer to question number 1 for each breed. When the answer is no, use the scissors to snip out a wedge, cutting away the edge of the card at the hole. When the answer is yes, do not cut out the hole.

Now let's say someone wants to buy a dog but would prefer a breed that would make a good guard dog. Stack the cards with the names of the dog breeds facing up. Slip the pipe cleaner or knitting needle through the holes next to the number 5, let go of the stack, and shake. The cards for those breeds that aren't known for being good guard dogs will drop out of the stack. The cards left hanging on the pipe cleaner will be those breeds with a reputation for being good guard dogs.

To carry this selection process further, let's say that the guard dog should preferably be short-haired. Sort the stack of guard dogs by inserting the probe in hole number 3 and shaking. Only those with naturally short hair will be left.

Most Popular Dog Survey

Which breed of dog is most popular in your community? Take a survey to find out. Ask at least 20 people who are dog owners what breed they own and write down that information. List "mixed breed" for any dog that is not a definite pure breed. Draw a bar graph similar to the sample graph below. Like stacking blocks, color in one square in the column for a specific breed for each person owning that type of dog. When your bar graph is complete, you'll be able to tell at a glance which breed is the most popular, second most popular, and so forth.

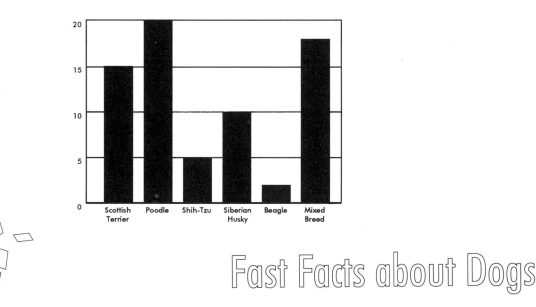

Fast Facts about Dogs

The tallest dogs are Great Danes and Irish wolfhounds. It's not unusual for these dogs to be more than 39 inches tall at the shoulder. These are not the heaviest dogs, though. Saint Bernards hold that record, usually weighing between 150 to 180 pounds when full grown.

When a dog licks its wounds, it's actually helping itself get well. A dog's saliva, the liquid produced in its mouth, contains a natural germ killer.

Not all dogs are able to bark. One breed that can't, called basenji, is sometimes used as a hunting dog. Maybe these dogs are especially good at sneaking up on game animals.

Many dogs have a better sense of smell than people do. In fact, bloodhounds are so naturally good at tracking smells, they're often used to find criminals and missing persons.

How Many Penguins?

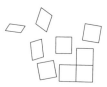

How many penguins are in this picture? Definitely a lot! Take a close look because every one of the little black-and-white bodies is a penguin. Of course, you could count the penguins, but that would be a lot of work and probably would take you a very long time. You'll be happy to know that there's an easy way to estimate, or make a good guess at, how many penguins are in this picture. You'll find instructions for how to do this on the next page.

You'll need a large-size transparent plastic storage bag, transparent tape, a permanent marking pen, a ruler, and scissors. Work on a surface that tape won't mar. Smooth the bag out flat and use tape to anchor the edges. Then, with the marking pen and ruler, make dots at 2-inch intervals from left to right along the bottom edge and from the bottom corner to the top corner along one side edge of the bag. Repeat, marking the top and opposite side edge in the same way. Now draw horizontal lines one at a time by laying the ruler across the plastic to connect dots that are directly opposite each other. Do the same thing to draw vertical lines. Trim off any part of the side or top of the bag that doesn't have full 2-inch-square blocks.

When this plastic grid is ready, lay it over the photo. Pick three squares—one that's nearly full of penguins, one that appears to have very few, and any other square. Count the number of penguins in each square. Divide the sum by 3 to find the average number of penguins in these squares. Now use this to guess how many penguins are in the whole picture.

Check that number by estimating. To make an estimate, count the number of complete blocks covering the photo, including the ones in which you counted the penguins. Multiply the total number of blocks by the average number of penguins per block. The result you get will be a pretty good estimate of the total number of penguins in the photo.

Now that you know an easy way to estimate large numbers of things, here's another challenge for you. How many coins are in this picture?

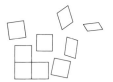

Okay, ready for some even tougher estimating challenges? Here are two:

1. How many names are in your local phone book?

2. How many raisins are in a box of raisin cereal? If possible, check several different brands to see which has the most raisins.

You won't be able to use the grid you prepared to solve either of these challenges, but the same basic technique will work. When you think you've figured out how to make these estimates, read on.

1. To estimate the number of names in your local phone book, count the number of names on any one page that's completely full of entries. Next, count the number of pages in the phone book, including the one on which you counted the names. Then multiply the number of names on one page times the number of pages in the phone book.

• Do you think every page has the same number of names?

• Did you guess that it's best to check at least three samples and compute an average?

• How can you be sure the page you're checking is typical of the whole book?

2. To estimate the number of raisins in a box of raisin cereal, first measure out a 2-ounce sample (¼ of a cup is 2 ounces). Count how many raisins are in this sample and divide by 2 to get the number per ounce. Then check how many ounces of cereal are in the box and multiply this number by the number of raisins in 1 ounce.

• Do you think raisins settle to the bottom of the cereal box?

• How can you be sure the sample you're checking is typical of the whole box?

Which Dinosaur Was Running?

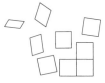

Look closely at the two photos showing dinosaur tracks. These are fossil footprints made a very long time ago when dinosaurs roamed the earth. The tracks were formed when the dinosaurs happened to cross a soft riverbank. Later, that soft material hardened into rock. Fossil tracks like the ones in the pictures below provide scientists with some clues about the dinosaurs that made them. According to Dr. James O. Farlow, an expert on dinosaur footprints, one thing the tracks reveal is whether the dinosaur was running or walking. Which of the sets of tracks shown here do you think shows the dinosaur was running? Why?

When you think you know the answer, read on.

The distance between a specific spot, such as the front tip, of a footprint on one side of an animal's body and the same spot on the next footprint on that same side is called a stride. If the dinosaur walked on all four feet, the trackway would be made up of two lines of footprints—those for the feet on the left side of the body and those for the feet on the right side. If the dinosaur walked on two feet, the tracks would form a single line. Then one stride would be formed by the distance between every other footprint or between two right or two left footprints.

According to Dr. Farlow, the average stride length for a walking dinosaur was about 5 to 7 times the length of one footprint. If the dinosaur was running, the stride length was as much as 15 to 20 times the footprint's length.

So which dinosaur was running? The one whose tracks are farther apart.

Checking Some Tracks of Your Own

Is the length of your stride different when you run than it is when you're walking?

To find out, you'll need to go to a large sandbox. Take along a rake and a measuring tape or yardstick. First, smooth the sand flat with the back of the rake. Next, walk across the sand. Measure the distance of one stride—the distance from the front tip of one right footprint to the front tip of the next right footprint; or the distance from the front tip of one left footprint to the front tip of the next left footprint. Repeat, measuring the distance between two other strides. Add up these 3 numbers and divide by 3 to find the average length of your stride when walking.

Now, smooth out the sand again and run across it. Repeat measuring three different strides. If the sandbox is small enough to cross in less than three strides, smooth the surface and run across again until you've collected the measurement of three running strides. Add up these numbers and divide by 3 as you did before to find the average.

Your stride will be greater when you're running. How much greater?

When Was This Photo Taken?

Take a close look at this photo of a spider's web. When do you think it was taken?

A. On a windy, cloudy evening?

B. About noon on a hot, sunny day?

C. On a cool, clear morning?

The dew clinging to the web is a clue. When you think you know the answer, read on. You'll also find out how you can predict when dew is likely to form.

Did you guess that the photo was taken on a cool, clear morning? Droplets of water called dew collect on something when a thin layer of moist air comes in contact with a surface cooler than the dew point. The dew point is the temperature at which water vapor begins to condense, or change from a gas to a liquid.

The conditions for dew to form are most often just right on a cool, clear morning. Clouds help trap the earth's heat, preventing the air temperature from dropping to the dew point, and the drying effect of winds also tends to reduce the likelihood of dew formation. Dew definitely won't develop during the hot, sunny, noontime hours. In fact, you've probably noticed dewdrops disappear as the sun rises and the day heats up.

You can predict when dew is likely to form if you have a hygrometer, an instrument that measures the amount of water vapor in the air. Through years of careful observations, people who study the weather have discovered that there is a relationship between the relative humidity and the dew point. Relative humidity

52

means the amount of moisture in the air compared to 100 percent, the total amount it could hold. As the relative humidity increases, the dew point temperature decreases. If the relative humidity is very high and the air feels cool—especially when the temperature drops at night—you can suspect dew is likely to form.

To make your own hygrometer, you'll need:

- a 3-pound-size plastic tub with a lid, such as margarine comes in
- sharp scissors
- 2 indoor/outdoor thermometers
- 2 large rubber bands
- piece of cotton shoelace (the kind that is a tube) about 6 inches long

Follow the steps to construct and use the hygrometer. You'll need to make a copy of the chart on page 54.

- Cut a slot about 2 inches above the bottom of one side of the tub. Stretch the two rubber bands around the tub, spacing one about 2 inches above the other.
- Slide the thermometers under the rubber bands. Position one next to the slot. Open one end of the shoelace and slip it over the bulb end of this thermometer. Push the free end of the shoelace through the slot so it lies on the bottom of the tub. Pour in enough water to cover the bottom of the tub and snap on the lid. Check the water level daily and add more as needed.
- When you want to check the relative humidity, place the hygrometer outdoors. Wait about 15 minutes; then read both the dry bulb and the wet bulb thermometers.
- Subtract the wet bulb reading from the dry bulb reading to find the number of degrees difference. The less moisture there is in the air, the faster the water will evaporate from the shoelace. The evaporation will cool the thermometer. There will be a greater difference between the wet and dry bulb readings when the relative humidity is low.
- Now place one finger on the dry bulb reading at the top of the Relative Humidity Chart. Find the number that shows the degrees difference along the side of the chart and place one finger of your other hand on this number. Then slide your finger at the top of the chart down and your finger on the side of the chart across until the two meet. The number where your fingers meet indicates the relative humidity, the percentage of water vapor in the air compared to the amount it could hold at that temperature.

RELATIVE HUMIDITY CHART

Dry-Bulb Temperature in °C/°F

Difference between Dry-Bulb and Wet-Bulb Temperature	5 / 41	6 / 43	7 / 45	8 / 46	9 / 48	10 / 50	11 / 52	12 / 54	13 / 55	14 / 57	15 / 59	16 / 61	17 / 62	18 / 64	19 / 66	20 / 68	21 / 70	22 / 72	23 / 73	24 / 75
1	86	86	87	87	88	88	89	89	90	90	90	90	90	91	91	91	92	92	92	92
2	72	73	74	75	76	77	78	78	79	79	80	81	81	82	82	83	83	83	84	84
3	58	60	62	63	64	66	67	68	69	70	71	71	72	73	74	74	75	76	76	77
4	45	48	50	51	53	55	56	58	59	60	61	63	64	65	65	66	67	68	69	69
5	33	35	38	40	42	44	46	48	50	51	53	54	55	57	58	59	60	61	62	62
6	20	24	26	29	32	34	36	39	41	42	44	46	47	49	50	51	53	54	55	56
7	7	11	15	19	22	24	27	29	32	34	36	38	40	41	43	44	46	47	48	49
8				8	12	15	18	21	23	26	27	30	32	34	36	37	39	40	42	43
9						6	9	12	15	18	20	23	25	27	29	31	32	34	36	37
10									7	10	13	15	18	20	22	24	26	28	30	31
11											6	8	11	14	16	18	20	22	24	26
12														7	10	12	14	17	19	20

Look Closely!

Which strip of paper is longer? When you think you know, read on.

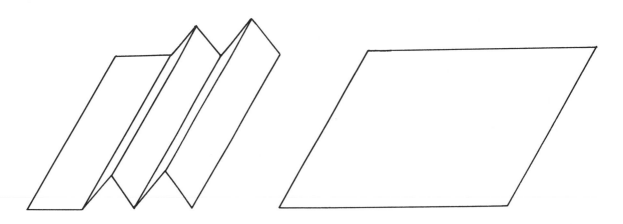

The two strips are identical—one has just been folded. Changing the shape of something doesn't alter its size, only its shape. If you aren't convinced, take two identical paper strips and fold one accordion style. To do that, fold over a flap at one end of the strip. Keep on folding until you reach the other end. Then spread the strip out, letting it naturally assume its new shape. You didn't cut off any of the strip, so even though some of the paper's length is pressed into zigzagging humps, it's still all there.

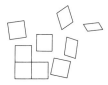

#

You've probably tackled the problem-solving challenge of finding your way through a maze. Now you can make your own mazes—ones that will be puzzles for you even though you've constructed them.

To successfully build your own mazes, follow these steps:

- Draw a box with an opening at one corner to allow entry into the maze and an opening at the opposite corner as an exit.

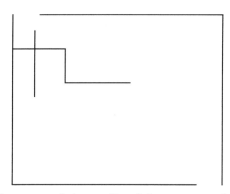

- Draw a line that touches one of the walls of the maze and only one wall. That line can be straight, angled, curved, or have any number of bends in it.
- Draw a second line that touches any point on this new line. Again it can be straight, angled, curved, or have bends in it. It may even cross the line where it originates. It must not touch or cross any other line, though.
- Continue to add lines to make the maze as complex as you like. You may begin each new line touching any line you like, but the new line must never come in contact with any other line.

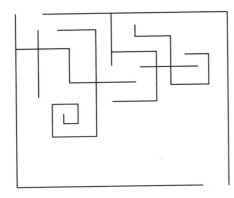

When you decide that the maze is complete, try it out. Can you find your way through from start to finish? Make other mazes to challenge yourself and to share with friends.

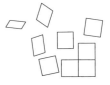

On the Job

Mathematics isn't just a subject to study in school, it's a skill people use every day. The following quotes will let you discover how people use mathematics in a variety of different careers. Each person responded to the question:

"What is the one key way in which you use mathematics on the job?"

Debra Lumpkin, kite designer (Lincoln City, Oregon): "The kite is an aircraft, and, like airplanes, there are three main forces at work on a kite—lift, gravity, and drag. Formulas exist for building kites. For example, the tail length should be 7 times the length of the kite's spine. I only use these formulas as guidelines, though, adjusting each kite by trial and error until it's both beautiful and graceful in flight."

Nolan Ryan, pitcher for the Texas Rangers (Dallas, Texas): "I'm involved in a number of areas in my life: baseball, ranching, and banking. Math is an important part of each and every one."

Ann W. Richards, governor of Texas (Austin, Texas): "Mathematics helps me read and decipher statistical data. I have to look at many types of reports with all types of statistics, and I need to be able to determine what the data really mean. Much of it can be misleading, if not looked at closely."

C. Moody Alexander, orthodontist (Dallas, Texas): "I use math to measure a person's teeth and to calculate the angles formed by the teeth, jaws, and facial lines. These measurements are important if I'm going to make sure the person's teeth are straight and that they have a beautiful smile."

Nizam Peters, diamond cutter (Fort Lauderdale, Florida): "Mathematics helps me precisely measure angles as I cut gems. When the angles are perfect, light is totally reflected, producing the maximum brilliance in a diamond."

Captain Stuart Grant, in charge of Station 20, Dallas Fire Department (Dallas, Texas): "Before we can begin to fight any fire, we have to figure how much water we will need. This is done by calculating the number of gallons of water per minute we need to pump. Without math skills it would be difficult for us to put out fires."

Dana Greiner, real estate agent (Atlanta, Georgia): "Mathematics is very important in everything a real estate agent does. The agent determines the value of the house and sets a sales price. When the house sells, the agent earns a percentage of the sales price. Besides being able to use a calculator and a computer, real estate agents must be able to multiply, divide, add, and subtract in their heads. They must be able to explain all of the numbers to their customers."

Tammy Jernigan, astronaut, National Aeronautics and Space Administration (Houston, Texas): "I use the problem-solving skills I learned in my math courses every day at work, including the days I spent in space. For example, during the de-orbit burn on STS-40, our crew used our math skills to ensure that our altitude was decreasing at the correct rate and that our engines were burning properly so that we could return safely to earth."

Congratulations!

Having solved all of these mysteries, you are now a mathematics supersleuth. But don't stop being curious and investigating. There's a world full of mysteries that need solving, and you've discovered new strategies for tackling puzzling situations.

The next time you go to the grocery store, check out the price of something available both by the pound and in prepackaged bags, such as potatoes. Can you figure out which is the better buy? Or go on a pattern hunt, looking at the arrangement of things, such as windows in office buildings, tree leaves on branches, and bricks on the sides of houses. Next time your family takes a trip, check the distance on the map and calculate how long it will take to reach your destination traveling at the speed limit. Make a list of possible stops and delays and compute a final arrival time.

Time how much of your favorite television programs are actually commercials. Even better, wonder whether or not a commercial claim is true and develop a way to test and measure that claim.

There's definitely a lot of action waiting for you. Be curious, and you'll soon be working on your next math mini-mystery!

Index